Daddy Pig Puts Up a Picture

Mummy Pig is going to visit Granny and Grandpa Pig.
She calls to tell them she is on her way.

Daddy Pig is staying at home with Peppa and George.
He has an important job to do.

Daddy Pig is going to put up a picture.
He is the DIY expert of the house.

"Are you sure you can do it?" asks Mummy Pig.
"Please don't make a mess."
"Ho! Ho! Ho!" laughs Daddy Pig.

As soon as Mummy Pig has gone,
Daddy Pig gets started.
"Stand back children, and watch a craftsman
at work," he says.

Daddy Pig finds
a nail to hang the
picture on. He gets
out his hammer.

"Don't break
the wall, Daddy,"
warns Peppa.

Daddy Pig hits the nail with the hammer. Thwack!
Now there are lots of big cracks in the wall.

"It's not meant to do that," says Daddy Pig.
"Oooh!" cries Peppa. "You have broken the wall!"

Daddy Pig decides to pull the nail out
and fill in the cracks.

Uh oh, Daddy Pig has pulled too hard.
Now he really has broken
the wall!

"Do you think Mummy will notice?" asks Peppa.
"I think she might," says Daddy Pig.

Daddy Pig has to mend the wall before
Mummy Pig comes home. Peppa and George
help him fill the hole with bricks.

Hee!
Hee!
Hee!

Daddy Pig fetches some
plaster. He spreads it all
over the bricks.
"There!" he chuckles.
"Easy as pie!"

The wall is looking
better already.

Daddy Pig opens a pot of green paint.
He paints all over the plaster.
"It's as good as new!" he chuckles.

Hooray!

Hooray!

The wall is mended.
But look at all the mess
Daddy Pig has made!

"Goodness me," says Daddy Pig.
"We'd better clean up before Mummy Pig
comes back."

Daddy Pig washes Peppa and George.
They haven't had a bath in the
daytime before!

Peppa vacuums the floor, while Daddy Pig
tidies up the tools.
"Hurry, Daddy!" says Peppa.

George watches at the window. "Mummy!"
Mummy Pig is walking up to the house!

"Hello!" says Mummy Pig.
"Why haven't you put up the picture?"
She quickly hangs it on the wall. "There!"

"That looked easy," gasps Peppa, "but when
you did it, Daddy, it looked really hard."
"Shh . . . don't tell anyone!" said Daddy Pig.